Arabelle

The bat with the most wonderful pink glasses

© 2013, Danielle R. Lindner
CreateSpace Publishing Company

A London Day School® Book – used under license by Rethinkinginc, LLC.
The London Day School name and logo are trademarks of SLD Holdings LLC

ISBN-13: 978-1490538006
ISBN-10: 1490538003

Arabelle the bat loved to curl up in bed
She would cling to the rafters
And hang down from her head

When the sun said hello
And away went the moon
Off to bed
Off to bed
Daddy would croon

But as soon as the moon took over the sky
Arabelle was up
Ready to fly

Arabelle's rainforest was the place she called home
A wonderful, colorful, wet place to roam
It was time to go looking for fruit and for berries
Arabelle loved mangoes, bananas and cherries

She's a fruit eating bat
As you most likely could tell
Who loved to eat fruit, the taste and the smell

She would fly through the night
And search in the trees
Finding mangoes and cherries
And bananas with ease

But then late one night
As she flew through the sky
She hit something hard and let out a cry

She thought she was heading
For a nice prickly pear
But all of a sudden a tree trunk was there

Ouch! She cried to her friends, Clive and Brie
What happened? They said
Did you hit a tree?

I did, she cried with a look of dismay
The pear was right there
The tree got in the way

I wanted to get a sweet, juicy bite
But my eyes must have tricked me
I'm losing my sight

The mangoes and grapefruits look blurry and small
Those figs and those dates…
I can't see them at all

You're blind as a bat!
Said her friend Marguerite
You flounder and stumble
Trip over your feet

So off Arabelle flew
To find mom and dad
She was scared and afraid that her eyes had gone bad

My eyes are too blurry
Everything's small
I bump into trees
I can't see at all

When looking for berries
Or bananas or figs
I fly into branches
Get tangled in twigs

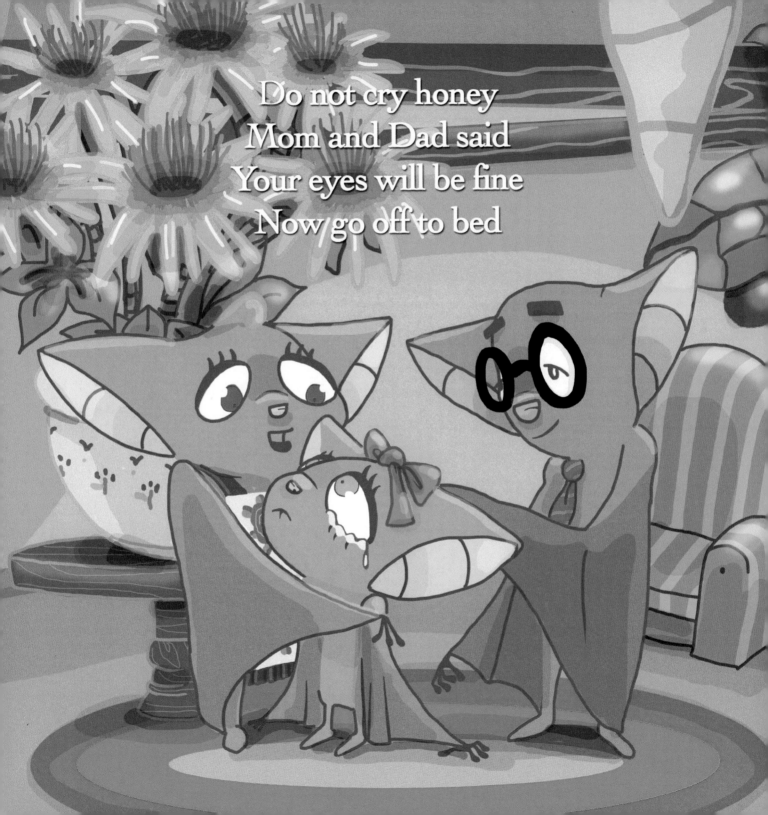

Do not cry honey
Mom and Dad said
Your eyes will be fine
Now go off to bed

The next day the sun
Came up and went down
But Arabelle stayed home
With tears and a frown

Don't worry dad said
All will be fine
I bought you some glasses
They are like mine

Glasses? Said Arabelle
What will they do?
They look sort of silly
I'll look just like you!

They will help you see mangoes, bananas and cherries
They will help you find figs, dates, grapefruits and berries

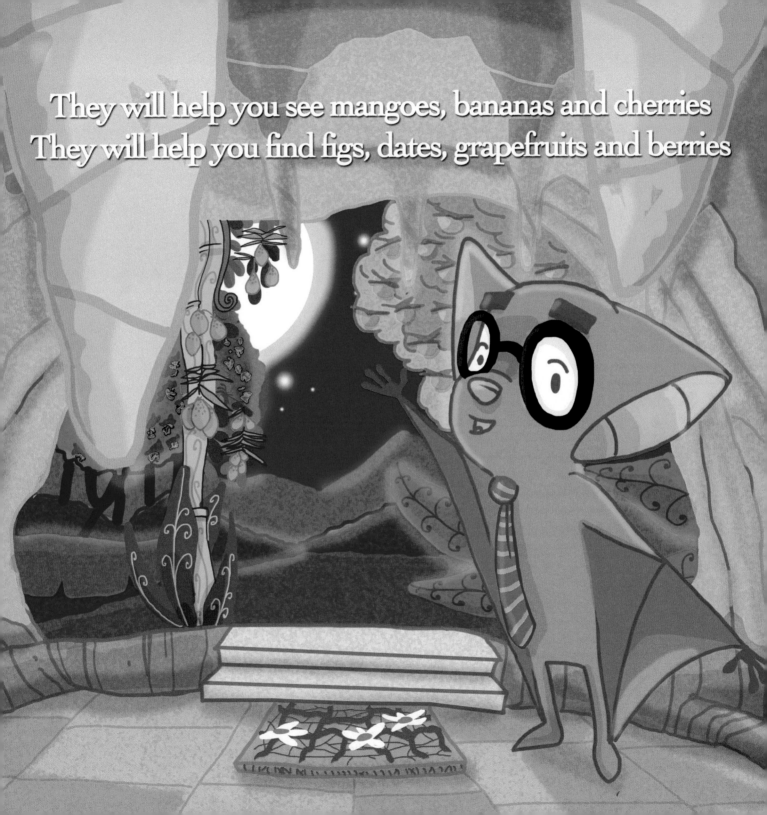

I will look silly
Not like Clive
Not like Brie
I don't want these glasses
I don't want to see

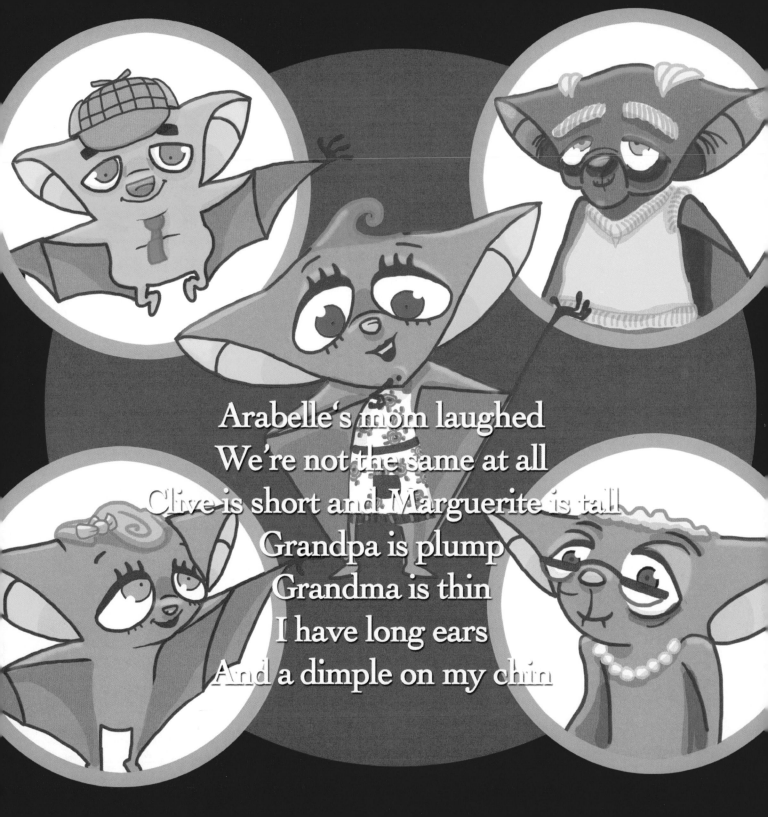

Arabelle's mom laughed
We're not the same at all
Clive is short and Marguerite is tall
Grandpa is plump
Grandma is thin
I have long ears
And a dimple on my chin

The thing that makes us special
Is how different we all are
Some of us see close
And some of us see far

Mommy flies slowly
And Daddy flies quickly
My skin is soft and Dad's is quite prickly

So Arabelle went to bed
To ponder and think
I guess I'd like glasses
Besides, they ARE pink!

The next night when all of the bats came to play
Everyone had something they wanted to say

We love your glasses
They're pink and so new
Brie and Clive wanted pink glasses too

These glasses are great
They really make me… me!
But the best part of all is how much I can see!

She loved her pink glasses
Her friends loved them too
And shortly thereafter
Clive got some in blue!

About the Author

Danielle Lindner, a member of the SCBWI (Society for Children's Book Writers and Illustrators), has a BA in Political Science and a Master of Arts in Teaching from Fairleigh Dickinson University. She is the founder of The London Day School® Preschool and Kindergarten Enrichment Academies.

The London Day School® was created by Ms. Lindner who saw a need for an enriching, challenging and socially engaging program for young children. Her schools and books provide a scaffolding approach to learning with a strong focus on character education.

Her books help children find their voice and become caring, nurturing and self-confident individuals. The first book in the series, Sofia the Snail, "The little snail that was afraid of the dark, "addresses a child's fear of nighttime darkness. Arabelle the Bat, "The bat with the most wonderful pink glasses," is the second in the series and addresses a child's fear of being "different and fitting in."

Ms. Lindner is also a contributor to The Alternative Press as the author of Nursery U, articles for parents and educators. She is the mother of two children and actively participates in community projects and programs that support and foster the wellness and joy of children.